WHA. IN THE WOODS?

story and pictures
by
June Goldsborough

Prentice-Hall, Inc., Englewood Cliffs, New Jersey

Printed in the United States of America ·J

Prentice-Hall International, Inc., London
Prentice-Hall of Australia, Pty. Ltd., North Sydney
Prentice-Hall of Canada, Ltd., Toronto
Prentice-Hall of India Private Ltd., New Delhi
Prentice-Hall of Japan, Inc., Tokyo

10 9 8 7 6 5 4 3 2 1

Library of Congress Cataloging in Publication Data
Goldsborough, June.
    What's in the woods?
    SUMMARY: Unable to identify a mysterious
creature, forest animals join forces to review the
clues it leaves behind.
    [1. Animals—Fiction] I. Title.
PZ7.G573Wh   [E]   76-10271
ISBN 0-13-955054-2

To Mother

Arise, and let us wander forth,
To yon old mill across the wolds;
For look, the sunset, south and north,
. . . Let us go.

                     Alfred Lord Tennyson

The animals knew there was something
strange in the woods.
The beaver saw it first. "It's woolly," he told
the chipmunk.

The deer said it was orange like the sun.

The earthworm claimed it was long like him. "And," said the fisher, "I've smelled it, and it is very interesting."

The grouse became so frightened that they hid in the thickest bushes. Only the sharp-eyed hawk could see them, but the inchworm stayed out of sight.

The jays called a warning through the woods.
The katydids nervously sang: "Katy-did, katy-
didn't, katy-did, katy-didn't."

The ladybug said, "I tried to walk over it, but it was too big. It's a mountain that moves." "Let's ask Bear to protect us," said the mouse. The nuthatch moved about the tree to get a better view.

The otter splashed to the bank. "What's going on?" he asked.
"It's a puzzle," the porcupine remarked.
The quails sat in a circle and worried.

When the rabbits heard about it they
scattered all over the woods.

The animals decided to take the problem to the owl who was old and wise.

"It looked harmless to me," said the snake. "I wouldn't be so sure," said the toad. "Let's go along."

Even the unicorn beetle came.
The animals chattered all at once, telling the
owl what they had seen.
"Your facts are unrealistic and unreliable,"
the owl said to them.
"But, of course, it could be a vicuna."
"What's that?" yelled the woodchuck.

"It is an ancient member of the camel family, native to South America," said the owl. "It would seem big to Ladybug, it is woolly and it is long. A most interesting animal, but not, to my knowledge, orange. If you will make an X on the spot where you encounter this creature, I will inspect it after my nap."
The yellow jackets flew off mad, and the bear slept through it all, "Z-Z-Z-Z-Z."

Just then the fox arrived.
"Oh look," said the beaver, "it's the fox!"
"He's woolly, he's long, he's interesting, he's
big," squeaked the mouse.
"And he is rather orange!" the rabbits
agreed.

The clever fox laughed, "Really, how can you
be so silly?
Your facts are right, but you just didn't get
the whole picture."